ARISE *in* ME

ARISE *in* ME

By Stella Rooks

For in Him we live and move and have our being,
as also some of your own poets have said,
'For we are also His offspring.'
Acts 17:28

A DAY-BY-DAY GUIDE TO HELP YOU MOVE FORWARD
IN TIMES OF DEPRESSION, ANXIETY AND TRIALS.

Published by

WORD PRODUCTIONS
PO BOX 11865 • ALBUQ. NM 87192 • WORDPRODUCTIONS.ORG

Arise In Me
By Stella Rooks
Copyright ©2013 by Stella Rooks

Published by **Word Productions LLC**
Albuquerque, NM 87192 USA

Printed in the United States of America.

ISBN: 978-0-9827998-7-1

All Scripture quotations in this book are from the New King James Version unless otherwise noted. Copyright ©1979, 1980, 1982 by Thomas Nelson, Inc. Used by permission. All rights reserved.

Scripture quotations marked (ESV) are from The Holy Bible, English Standard Version® (ESV®), copyright ©2001 by Crossway, a publishing ministry of Good News Publishers. Used by permission. All rights reserved.

To order additional books:
  Order from Desert Rose Creations:
  E-mail: stellarooks@gmail.com

  OR online nationally and internationally through Amazon at www.amazon.com

ACKNOWLEDGEMENTS

I want to thank my husband, James, who stood by my side as I expressed my compassion towards this book and the compassion I had towards individuals with depression and anxiety. He encouraged me to do and stay focused on it. I also want to thank my beautiful daughter Pamela, who also encouraged me. Always with her smiles, but always telling me, "Just do it, Mom! Don't be afraid." I would like to thank all my family and friends who prayed for this book and encouraged me with many kind words.

A special thank you to my Pastor, Ray Montoya, and his wife Sonia. They are always there to listen and pray. Thank you for your feedback on this book, your prayers and your encouragement.

Most importantly, I would like to thank my great God who, through His Son Jesus, gives me life. He alone gave me the desire to do this book and put it in my heart to reach out to those who wonder "Why am I alive?" "I can't move, I have no strength," and "I don't know why I am living." He alone gave me the strength to put this book together and provided for it to be completed. May all the glory go to God. He made me realize who

He is, how great He is, His love for me, His forgiveness, how compassionate toward me He is, how Righteous He is, how Holy he is. Through my trials I cried out and He drew me closer to Him and embraced me with His Love.

PREFACE

BEFORE YOU BEGIN

I would like to let you know that this book is a God-given tool for you to make an honest effort to walk out of depression and anxiety and press on to a far better life.

I can't relate to all of your issues in life that bring you to the point of depression and anxiety, nor can you relate to mine. For that matter, no one can relate to everyone's circumstances. But, what I can relate to is the symptoms of depression and anxiety. They are paralyzing, full of fear, worry and negative thoughts, to mention a few. I have experienced these symptoms sometimes for weeks or months at a time, and sometimes for years.

As a non-Christian, I had a very difficult time dealing with these illnesses. I did not know what they were; I did not know what to do. There were many frightful times. I wanted to die, and then I didn't. My mind never shut down. My family didn't know what I was going through; I had no one to help me.

As a Christian, I was able to seek God with all my heart, soul, and mind. I began to be extremely desperate for Him. I searched for Him daily in His Word and through prayer; He walked me through some tough times.

Depression and Anxiety are not from God, but from the
enemy. He would love to keep you away from experiencing a full life in Jesus Christ, full of peace and joy
and from a love that surpasses all understanding.

We have to be careful about what we do with our
depression and anxiety. Do we seek Jesus and a life
that has meaning, or do we stay in the same place
where life has no meaning? Be careful not to make
the choice of staying where you're at; this means that
you are accustomed to your life. Are you addicted to
depression and anxiety? Do you freak out when there
is some joy in your life and then wait for something
bad to happen to bring you down again, because you
don't deserve the joy?

When God gives you joy, take it for what it is and enjoy
it. He wants us to have a joyful life through His Son,
Jesus Christ.

There is no better way to walk away from depression
and anxiety than to walk out of it with Jesus Christ. He
loves you and comforts you.

Make a choice to do this book for one month. You have
opened it to this point, keep turning the pages to see
where God leads you.

In Him we LIVE and MOVE and have our being...

In Acts 17:28a we read "for in Him we live and move
and have our being, as also some of your own poets
have said."

We **LIVE** because…He breathed life into us.

In whose hand is life of every living thing, and the breath of all mankind. (Job 12:10)

The Spirit of God has made me, and the breath of the Almighty gives me life. (Job 33:4)

For You formed my inward parts; You have covered me in my mother's womb. I will praise You, for I am fearfully and wonderfully made; marvelous are your works, and that my soul knows very well. (Psalm 139:13-14)

We **MOVE** because…He strengthens us.

God is our refuge and strength, a very present help in trouble. (Psalm 46:1)

He gives power to the weak, and to those who have no might He increases strength. (Isaiah 40:29)

But those who wait on the LORD shall renew their strength; they shall mount up with wings like eagles, they shall run and not be weary, they shall walk and not faint. (Isaiah 40:31)

We **HAVE OUR BEING** because…
He sustains us daily with His love.

By You I have been upheld from birth; You are
He who took me out of my mother's womb.
My praise shall be continually of You.
(Psalm 71:6)

In Psalm 3:7a we read: "Arise, O LORD; Save me,
O my God!" Hence, the title of the book *Arise in Me*.
Jesus Christ is the whole, the sum of our lives. In Him,
we have life for eternity, strength to press on, and we
come to realize that we exist for His glory.

"Just as You rise up the sun everyday,
Let your Son arise in me.
Then I will live, move, and have my being."

This was one of my prayers to God, as I one day started
to recognize the symptoms of depression and anxiety
that I had experienced for years before becoming a
Christian.

Prior to becoming a Christian, trials of many sorts in-
cluding finances, loss of a loved one, life-threatening
illnesses, marriage problems, and of course SIN itself
led to stress which led to my depression and anxiety. At
times, shopping and gambling became a way of dealing with issues of life...instant gratification. But, they
can also lead to depression and anxiety. What a vicious
cycle. As I suffered through depression and anxiety
my mind was in total confusion. I wanted to die and
then I had the fear of dying. At times all I wanted to do

was sleep and then I was so irritable I couldn't sleep. My mind was going 24/7. My thoughts were of everything I could possibly think of...you know, the guilt, regrets, the if's, the would-have's, should-have's, the could-have's. Oh yes...the who is liking me and who isn't, caring about what everyone thinks. Many times I filled my mind with things that weren't even going to happen. Filling my mind with the past—while trying to cope with the present—all the while trying to figure out the future. I felt sad and felt hopeless. I would be awakened by strong heart palpitations that felt like they were coming out of my chest. I would be awakened by my mind because thoughts were running rampant. I felt exhausted. I thought of suicide. I felt the inadequacy and the fear of not being able to accomplish anything. I felt muscle aches. I felt like a walking time-bomb ready to explode. I felt the loneliness, yet at times I didn't want to be around anyone. I despised the image I saw when I looked in the mirror. I wondered, "Who is that person who looks so sad, hopeless and pale?" I felt so helpless. My life meant nothing and I felt so **DEFEATED!**

I saw no color. The depression and anxiety had darkened my world. I felt like a robot just going through the motions. My mind was so overrun and polluted by negative thoughts. I didn't want to take drugs for my symptoms and I was alone and didn't know what to do; so I cried out to God. I knew He was out there, somewhere...He answered. He became my personal Lord and Savior.

As trials and circumstances arose in my life again, I started to feel the symptoms again. I couldn't believe it. I am a Christian; how can this happen? I was not leading a sinful life but trying to live a life pleasing to God. Then I realized it was once again stress and worry that were leading to the familiar symptoms. My mind full of negative thoughts again, only this time I knew what to do. I cried out to God, "Arise in Me" as I read His word. "Increase in me that I may decrease. Fill me with thoughts of You and take my thoughts of me. I want to live, I want to move, and I want to exist for You."

FATHER, HELP ME TO BE ABOUT
YOUR BUSINESS...

This was another important prayer. I was reading the Bible and I read Luke 2:49, "And He said to them, 'Why did you seek Me? Did you not know that I must be about My Father's business?'" Wow, this was what God revealed to me: I realized that I needed to be about my Father's business instead of my own business. I needed to set my mind upon Him and not my circumstances. I needed to seek Him in my mind through reading His Word and through serving Him. I also needed to purpose in my mind to serve others and not myself.

I made a decision to seek God with all my heart, all my strength, and all my mind, one day at a time. I began to seek Him in His Word. I began praying to Him like never before, and I began singing to Him like never before. I began to worship Him for being Holy, Righteous, and Just. I was so desperate for Him I began to praise Him for my life and for the things He was doing in it. I would relate His creations with things, like the sun which reminded me of His love for me in that He should desire to give me light. The mountains reminded me of His power and strength. His detail on the mountains reminded me of His detailed work in me. I began to see His grace and all the good things He'd given me. I began to thank Him for phone calls of encouragement, texts, smiles, hugs, walks, and drives from anywhere to any place. He always orchestrated beautiful things in my life, when I needed them the most.

As I focused more on Him, through reading, praying and serving, I found that I didn't have the time to focus on my circumstances anymore. I realized that God would carry me through them, deliver me out of them, and that He was faithful to keep His promises. As I also focused on the needs of others, which is being about my Father's business, I was able to start experiencing less negative thoughts and more wonderful things of God.

It is so awesome now to wake up in the morning with God and Jesus on my mind in the form of His Word or a song. I was able to come to the end of the day and know that He was with me all day. To be able to set my mind upon Jesus when I go to bed is priceless. My life means something... I have **VICTORY**!

In Short:
THE FLOW CHART OF MY LIFE

Before Jesus Christ

Trials
Financial, Death of a loved one,
SIN, Job Loss, Marriage Problems,
Life-Threatening Illnesses.

Stress

Anxiety
Worry, fear of dying, paralyzed, couldn't
get myself to do anything, feeling of
inadequacy, very emotional, sensitive,
fatigued, muscle tension, loss of sleep,
twitching, irritability, sweating and heart
palpitations, negative thoughts 24/7, doubt.

Depression
Hopelessness, darkness, numbness; slept
all day; no energy, sadness, guilt, low
self-image; inability to think, concentrate,
make decisions; thoughts of death, suicide;
negative thoughts 24/7.

My Answers

Addictions
Shopping, gambling and anything
to take my mind off of things.

Pills & Psychiatrist

After JESUS CHRIST

GOD's Only Answer
Surrender All
= JESUS CHRIST

Jesus Christ
Peace, strength, restful nights,
able to accomplish things,
trusting in God for all things.

Jesus Christ
Hope, light, energy, desire to
do things, able to think more
clearly, thankful thoughts, taking
mind off of myself; desire to live.

Jesus Christ
Being a good servant with
What I had.

Jesus Christ
Reading His Word, Praying,

I was able to overcome depression and anxiety, gambling, and shopping and have peace and joy by setting my mind upon Jesus, one day at a time.

This guidebook is designed to direct you to take small steps to seek Jesus one day at a time. But, first you have to make that decision in your heart. You have to want change. You have to want Him in all parts of your life.

You can CHOOSE to...

Have **Faith** =
Trust in God and His Word,
Believe in His Son JESUS CHRIST
And **Fight** =
Prayer & Strength to PRESS ON.
And **Flourish** = ability to THRIVE to GROW
and to become dependent on GOD

Or you can CHOOSE to...

Have **Fear** = the enemy, being afraid

And **Fret** = worry, discontent, irritable, tiresome,

And **Fall** = falling into SIN, into anxiety,
into depression and into addictions.
Into outer darkness.

 This is completely up to you. No one can make this choice for you. It is totally a commitment to be made by you to make every effort to seek God and take steps to healing. This choice must come from your HEART, so check yours.

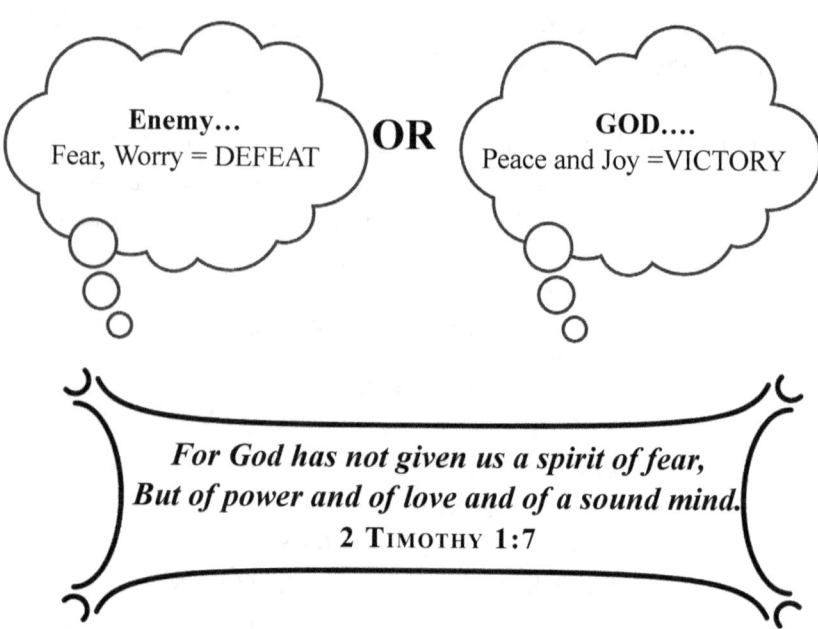

God can govern your thoughts and
take your mind off your
Circumstances,
Or
Your circumstances can govern your thoughts,
and take your mind off of
GOD

My prayer is that you to choose to
connect your heart with God's.

FIRST THINGS FIRST

First, if you are not a Believer, simply give your heart
to Jesus and put your trust in HIM.

Romans 10:9-10 tells us "that if we confess with our
mouth the Lord Jesus and believe in our heart that God
has raised Him from the dead, we will be saved. For
with the heart one believes unto righteousness, and
with the mouth confession is made unto salvation.

Prayer:
*Dear Jesus, I know that I am a sinner and I need your
forgiveness. I ask that you forgive me. I know that
You gave Your life and that you died for my sins. I ask
that You come and live in my heart and take charge of
my life. I ask that You become my personal Lord and
Savior so that I may follow You all the days of my life.
In Jesus' name, Amen.*

God tells us in His Word...

*I will give you a new heart
and put a new spirit within you;
I will take the heart of stone out of your flesh
and give you a heart of flesh.
I will put My Spirit within you
and cause you to walk in My statues and
you will keep My judgments and do them.*
(Ezekiel 36:26-27)

He promises us a new heart, and with that new heart a desire to seek Him with all that we have. We then have the strength to fill our minds with things of Him and not of ourselves.

David cried out to God...

Search me, O God, and know my heart;
try me, and know my anxieties;
And see if there is any wicked way in me,
And lead me in the way everlasting.
(Psalm 139:23-24)

Cry out to Jesus, He will answer!

Jesus told us that in this world we would have tribulations: *"These things I have spoken to you, that in Me you may have peace. In the world you will have tribulations; but be of good cheer, I have overcome the world"* (John 16:33).

HOWEVER...

Jesus wants us to be of good cheer;
because He overcame, we also can be overcomers.

Finally, Brethren, whatever things are TRUE,
Whatever things are NOBLE,
Whatever things are JUST,
Whatever things are PURE,
Whatever things are LOVELY,
Whatever things are of GOOD REPORT,
If there is any VIRTUE,
And if there is anything PRAISEWORTHY,
Meditate on these things.

The things which you learned and received and
Heard and saw in me, these do, and the
God of peace will be with you.
(Philippians 4:8-9)

These scriptures helped me tremendously to overcome my down times. I found that as I meditated on God and His grace and all the good things in my life, He quickly changed my thinking from negative to thankful thoughts. I went from complaining to being thankful; from being unhappy to being joyful; from not being content to being content in all things. 1 John 4:18-19: "There is no fear in love; but perfect love casts out fear, because fear involves torment. But he who fears has not been made perfect in love. We love Him because he first loved us." Focus on His love and not fear. Fear is the opposite of Faith.

How This Book Works...

This guidebook is to help you focus on God one day at a time; focus on His goodness and not your circumstance(s). When you focus on Jesus it helps you take your mind off yourself. While your focus is on the one true God and His goodness, He will guide you to deal with your issues one day at a time. He reveals His love for you in so many ways. You don't have to try to deal with all your issues at once and feel overwhelmed and stay in the same rot that you are in.

Each day is formatted to help you set your mind on the things of God and includes the following:

1. READING & PRAYING = A SPECIFIC WORD

When you read God's Word and pray you will find what the meaning of that word is. Each one of these words is the opposite of what I felt when I had my depression and anxiety. Then you will have scriptures that relate to that word. This is to encourage you to read and pray about what God is revealing to you through His scriptures. Example: Day 1 Reading & Praying = Love. When you read and pray you will find how much God loves you and how much we need to love Him.

2. I WILL SET MY THOUGHTS ON HIS WORD

This is an example of praying God's Word back to Him. It is poetic, but I love the way Christian artists write songs. They are very poetic. What better way to sing back to our God, but through His Word.

3. TAKE A MOMENT TO PRAY GOD'S WORD BACK TO HIM AND ASK HIM TO REVEAL THINGS TO YOU.

4. THE HEART CHECK, CONNECTING YOUR HEART TO GOD'S—

This is very crucial to moving forward. Always examine yourself and ask God to search your heart and mind and to reveal things you need to confess and change. Making sure you are in tune with God is being in His will and glorifying Him.

5. LASTLY, 5 THINGS I AM THANKFUL FOR ARE...

This a great exercise for your mind. Despite my circumstances I sat down and wrote things I was thankful for. These really helped me to focus on good things and not my negative thoughts. Instantly, I was able to set my mind on God and not my circumstances. He is good and blesses us in many ways. Writing down the things I was thankful for help me to praise Him for things I would take for granted. The simple little things like... having a cup of coffee with my husband, a phone call from my daughter, a text from someone encouraging me, a hug or smile from someone. His works encouraged me to think about Him. Pray and He will reveal little things that can make a big difference in your day.

Depression and Anxiety and our circumstances can make us feel like we are imprisoned. But, I love that Paul didn't let His imprisonment stop him from praising God. Acts 16:25 says, "But, at midnight Paul and Silas were praying and singing hymns to God and the prisoners were listening to them." Read, pray, and sing hymns to God one day at a time and He will guide you out of the darkness into His marvelous light.

NOTE:

At any given time throughout each day, should the enemy start to fill your mind with negative thoughts, immediately start to fill your mind with things of God.

EXAMPLE:

First, ask Jesus to take your thoughts captive. Then... on Day 1 when the enemy starts to fill your mind with negative thoughts you will fill your mind with the Reading and Praying = Love. You will meditate on the scriptures about Love and on your prayer regarding Love.

You will meditate on the things you need to Put Off
and to Put On, and then you will meditate on the things
you are thankful for. You will have VICTORY in Jesus.

DAY 1

READING & PRAYING

= *Love*

For God so loved the world
that He gave His only begotten Son,
that whoever believes in Him
should not perish but have everlasting life.
JOHN 3:16

I love those who love me, and those who seek me
diligently will find me.
PROVERBS 8:17

" 'And you shall love the LORD your God with all
your heart, with all your soul,
And with all your mind, and with all your strength.'
This is the first commandment."
MARK 12:30

Pause and take a moment to pray about God's love towards you. Ask Him to reveal things to you.

I Will Set My Thoughts on His Word

I want to believe in Your Son, that I may have life. LORD God, help me to love You with all that I am.

Fill me with Your love and give me Your strength, so I may seek You always and Your love I will understand.

MY PRAYER TO GOD

_____
_____
_____
_____

God revealed to me what I must PUT OFF:
_____

And what I must PUT ON:
_____

5 THINGS I AM THANKFUL FOR

_____
_____
_____
_____
_____
_____
_____

DAY 2

READING & PRAYING

= *Forgiveness*

❦

*For You, Lord, are good, and ready to forgive,
and abundant in mercy to all who call upon You.*
PSALM 86:5

❖ ❖ ❖

*To Him all the prophets bear witness that
everyone who believes in Him receives
forgiveness of sins through His name.*
ACTS 10:43 ESV

❖ ❖ ❖

*If we confess our sins, He is faithful and just
to forgive us our sins and to cleanse us
from all unrighteousness.*
1 JOHN 1:9

Pause and take a moment to pray about God's forgiveness. Ask Him to reveal things to you.

I Will Set My Thoughts on His Word

Jesus, I will call upon You for You are good and full of mercy.
I confess my sins and ask for Your forgiveness.
I believe in You and know that You are faithful.
Only through Your name am I cleansed from unrighteousness.
Your forgiveness cannot not be comprehended.
But, forgive me, Jesus, my heart is in need of being mended.

MY PRAYER TO GOD

_____
_____
_____
_____

God revealed to me what I must PUT OFF:
_____

And what I must PUT ON:
_____

5 THINGS I AM THANKFUL FOR

_____
_____
_____
_____
_____
_____
_____

DAY 3

READING & PRAYING

= *Peace*

For God is not the author of confusion, but of peace.
1 CORINTHIANS 14:33A

❖ ❖ ❖

Be anxious for nothing, but in everything by prayer and supplication, with thanksgiving, let your requests be made known to God; and the peace of God, which surpasses all understanding, will guard your hearts and minds through Christ Jesus.
PHILIPPIANS 4:6-7

❖ ❖ ❖

You will keep him in perfect peace, whose mind is stayed on You, because he trusts in You.

ISAIAH 26:3

❖ ❖ ❖

In the multitude of my anxieties within me, Your comforts delight my soul.
PSALM 94:19

Pause and take a moment to pray about God's peace. Ask Him to reveal things to you.

I Will Set My Thoughts on His Word

I do not have peace, my mind is a mess.
I am consumed with a multitude of worries and distressed.
Allow me to experience that perfect peace, and help me to focus on Jesus Christ, from whom I am blessed.

MY PRAYER TO GOD

_____
_____
_____
_____

God revealed to me what I must PUT OFF:
_____

And what I must PUT ON:
_____

5 THINGS I AM THANKFUL FOR

_____
_____
_____
_____
_____
_____
_____

DAY 4

READING & PRAYING

= *Faith*

*But without faith it is impossible to please Him,
for he who comes to God must believe that He is,
and that He is a rewarder of those
who diligently seek Him.*
HEBREWS 11:6

❖ ❖ ❖

*But the Lord is faithful, who will establish you
and guard you from the evil one.*
2 THESS. 3:3

❖ ❖ ❖

*So Jesus said to them, "Because of your unbelief;
for assuredly, I say to you, if you have faith as a
mustard seed, you will say to this mountain, 'Move
from here to there', and it will move; and nothing
will be impossible for you."*
MATTHEW 17:20

Pause and take a moment to pray about God's faithfulness and your faith. Ask Him to reveal things to you.

I Will Set My Thoughts on His Word

Take away the faith that I have which is in myself.
Give me the faith of a mustard seed
So I can trust in You.
I believe that You will protect me from the evil one.
Strengthen my faith that
nothing shall be impossible for me to do.

MY PRAYER TO GOD

_____
_____
_____
_____

God revealed to me what I must PUT OFF:
_____

And what I must PUT ON:
_____

5 THINGS I AM THANKFUL FOR

_____
_____
_____
_____
_____
_____

DAY 5

READING & PRAYING

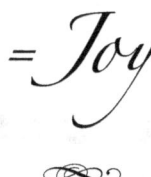

But let all those rejoice who put their trust in You;
let them ever shout for joy because You defend them;
let those also who love Your name be joyful in You.

PSALM 5:11

❖ ❖ ❖

You will show me the path of life;
in Your presence is fullness of joy;
at Your right hand are pleasures forevermore.

PSALM 16:11

❖ ❖ ❖

"These things I have spoken to you, that My joy
remain in you, and that your joy may be full."

JOHN 15:11

Pause and take a moment to pray about God's joy in your life. Ask Him to reveal things to you.

I Will Set My Thoughts on His Word

Although my heart is not full of joy, but of doubt,
Let me be in Your presence at the moment I shout.
Let Your joy, oh great Defender, remain in me forevermore.
As I walk through life; Your joy shall make me soar.

MY PRAYER TO GOD

God revealed to me what I must PUT OFF:

And what I must PUT ON:

5 THINGS I AM THANKFUL FOR

DAY 6

READING & PRAYING

= *Sound Mind*

For God has not given us a spirit of fear,
but of power and of love and of a sound mind.
2 TIM. 1:7

❖ ❖ ❖

And do not seek what you should eat or what you
should drink, nor have an anxious mind.
LUKE 12:29

❖ ❖ ❖

I sought the Lord, and He heard me,
And delivered me from all my fears.
PSALM 34:4

Pause and take a moment to pray about God's gift of a
sound mind. Ask Him to reveal things to you.

I Will Set My Thoughts on His Word

When I am afraid and full of fear,
I will call upon You to fill me with Your love and power.

Instill in me a mind that is sound and untroubled—
For You are my strong Tower.

MY PRAYER TO GOD

_____

_____

_____

_____

God revealed to me what I must PUT OFF:

_____

And what I must PUT ON:

_____

5 THINGS I AM THANKFUL FOR

_____

_____

_____

_____

_____

_____

DAY 7

READING & PRAYING

= *Humility*

A man's pride will bring him low,
but the humble in spirit will retain honor.
PROVERBS 29:23

But He gives more grace. Therefore He says:
"God resists the proud, but gives grace to the humble."
...Humble yourselves in the sight of
the Lord, and he will lift you up.
JAMES 4:6, 10

And being found in appearance as a man,
He humbled Himself and became obedient
to the point of death, even the death of the cross.
PHILIPPIANS 2:8

Please take a moment to pray about God's Son, Jesus, and His obedience and humility and yours. Ask Him to reveal things to you.

I Will Set My Thoughts on His Word

*I am a prideful person and
I like to walk with my head held tall.
Being right did not matter, it needed to be my way
...or no way at all.
Make me obedient as Jesus was when He obeyed Your call.
Remove my pride and humble me; to my knees I fall.*

MY PRAYER TO GOD

_____
_____
_____
_____

God revealed to me what I must PUT OFF:
_____
And what I must PUT ON:
_____

5 THINGS I AM THANKFUL FOR

_____
_____
_____
_____
_____
_____
_____

DAY 8

READING & PRAYING

= *Strength*

The LORD is my strength and my shield;
My heart trusted in Him, and I am helped;
therefore my heart greatly rejoices and
with my song I will praise Him.
PSALM 28:7

❖ ❖ ❖

He gives power to the weak, and to those
who have no might He increases strength.
ISAIAH 40:29

❖ ❖ ❖

I can do all things through Christ
who strengthens me.
PHILIPPIANS 4:13

Pause and take a moment to pray about God's
strength. Ask Him to reveal things to you.

I Will Set My Thoughts on His Word

I am overpowered by my weaknesses,
But You are my strength and my shield.

I shall rejoice and sing a song of praise to You,
My heart and trust to You I yield.

MY PRAYER TO GOD

_____

_____

_____

_____

God revealed to me what I must PUT OFF:

_____

And what I must PUT ON:

_____

5 THINGS I AM THANKFUL FOR

_____

_____

_____

_____

_____

_____

READING & PRAYING

= *Loving God Loving Others*

So he answered and said, " 'You shall love
the LORD your God with all your heart,
with all your soul, with all your strength,
and with all your mind' and
'your neighbor as yourself.' "
LUKE 10:27

❖ ❖ ❖

I, therefore, the prisoner of the Lord,
beseech you to walk worthy of the calling
with which you were called,
with all lowliness and gentleness,
with longsuffering,
bearing with one another in love.
EPHESIANS 4:1-2

Pause and take a moment to pray about loving God and loving others. Ask Him to reveal things to you.

I Will Set My Thoughts on His Word

LORD God, it seems impossible to love You and others...
When I don't even love myself.
Help me to love You and my neighbor
As You have loved me.
I will love You with all my heart, strength, mind and soul.
May my love for You be displayed for all the world to see.

MY PRAYER TO GOD

_____
_____
_____
_____

God revealed to me what I must PUT OFF:
_____

And what I must PUT ON:
_____

5 THINGS I AM THANKFUL FOR

_____
_____
_____
_____
_____
_____
_____

DAY 10

READING & PRAYING

= *Hope*

"For I know the thoughts that I think toward you,"
says the LORD, "thoughts of peace and not of evil,
to give you a future and a hope."
JEREMIAH 29:11

❖ ❖ ❖

"For My thoughts are not your thoughts, nor are your
ways My ways," says the LORD. "For as the heavens
are higher than the earth, so are My ways higher than
your ways, and my thoughts than your thoughts."
ISAIAH 55:6-9

❖ ❖ ❖

Now may the God of hope fill you with all joy and
peace in believing, that you may abound in hope
by the power of the Holy Spirit.
ROMANS 15:13

Pause and take a moment to pray about God's hope and
thoughts towards you. Ask Him to reveal things to you.

I Will Set My Thoughts on His Word

I have no hope for I cannot see past today;
Tomorrow will only bring the same.
Let me call upon You while You are near;
You pardon my sins and wipe them clear.
Your thoughts towards me are higher than the sky...
I shall be rich in hope and like an eagle I shall fly.

MY PRAYER TO GOD

_____

_____

_____

_____

God revealed to me what I must PUT OFF:

_____

And what I must PUT ON:

_____

5 THINGS I AM THANKFUL FOR

_____

_____

_____

_____

_____

_____

DAY 11

READING & PRAYING

= *Encouragement*

❧

"Fear not, for I am with you; be not dismayed,
for I am your God. I will strengthen you, yes,
I will help you. I will uphold you with
My righteous right hand."
ISAIAH 41:10

❖ ❖ ❖

"I am the vine, you are the branches.
He who abides in Me, and I in him, bears much fruit;
for without Me you can do nothing."
JOHN 15:5

❖ ❖ ❖

And let us not grow weary while doing good,
for in due season we shall reap if we do not lose heart.
GALATIANS 6:9

Pause and take a moment to pray about abiding in Jesus Christ. Ask Him to reveal things to you.

I Will Set My Thoughts on His Word

My heart and mind are full of fear, worries, and sorrow.
However, You are my God and my help today and tomorrow.
You will carry me and be my Guide,
And in You I shall abide.

MY PRAYER TO GOD

God revealed to me what I must PUT OFF:

And what I must PUT ON:

5 THINGS I AM THANKFUL FOR

READING & PRAYING

= *Regeneration*

Therefore, if anyone is in Christ, he is a new creation;
old things have passed away; behold,
all things have become new.
2 CORINTHIANS 5:17

For we are His workmanship created in Christ Jesus for
good works, which God prepared beforehand
that we should walk in them.
EPHESIANS 2:10

If indeed you have heard Him and have been taught by Him,
as the truth is in Jesus: that you put off, concerning your
former conduct, the old man which grows corrupt
according to the deceitful lusts, and be renewed
in the spirit of your mind, and that you put on
the new man which was created according to God
in true righteousness and holiness.
EPHESIANS 4:21-24

Pause and take a moment to pray about God's salvation.
Ask Him to reveal things to you.

I Will Set My Thoughts on His Word

A brand new start is not something I could have imagined.
The old things are all I could ponder.
You are a God that heals, restores, and makes whole.
You give gifts of life and salvation; I am in great wonder.
Do not let me be the workmanship of my past, but,
Let me be Your new creation and in my salvation be steadfast.

MY PRAYER TO GOD

_____
_____
_____
_____

God revealed to me what I must PUT OFF:
_____

And what I must PUT ON:
_____

5 THINGS I AM THANKFUL FOR

_____
_____
_____
_____
_____
_____
_____

DAY 13

READING & PRAYING

= *Serving God*

❧

...But as for me and my house, we will serve the LORD
JOSHUA 24:15B

❖ ❖ ❖

*I beseech you therefore, brethren, by the mercies of God,
that you present your bodies a living sacrifice, holy,
acceptable to God, which is your reasonable service.*
ROMANS 12:1

❖ ❖ ❖

*And whatever you do, work heartily,
as for the Lord and not for men,
knowing that from the Lord
you will receive the reward of inheritance;
for you serve the Lord Christ.*
COLOSSIANS 3:23-24

Pause and take a moment to pray about serving God. Ask Him to reveal things to you.

I Will Set My Thoughts on His Word

Focused on my own wicked ways, serving You was not in my plans.
Great God of grace and mercy, accept me into Your hands.
To You daily I surrender all to present myself spotless and pure.
May I labor for Your eyes only, to receive the inheritance I am sure.
My household shall serve you today and in the future, I pray...
That my hands and feet will be Yours all day.

MY PRAYER TO GOD

_____
_____
_____
_____

God revealed to me what I must PUT OFF:
_____
And what I must PUT ON:
_____

5 THINGS I AM THANKFUL FOR

_____
_____
_____
_____
_____

READING & PRAYING

= Serving Others

"For I was hungry and you gave Me food;
I was thirsty and you gave Me drink; I was a stranger
and you took Me in; I was naked and you clothed Me;
I was sick and you visited Me;
I was in prison and you came to Me."
MATTHEW 25:35

❖ ❖ ❖

And the King will answer and say to them, "Assuredly,
I say to you, inasmuch as you did it to one of the
least of these My brethren, you did it to Me."
MATTHEW 25:40

❖ ❖ ❖

Let nothing be done through selfish ambition or
conceit, but in lowliness of mind let each esteem others
better than himself. Let each of you look out not only
for his own interests but also for the interests of others.
PHILIPPIANS 2:3-4

Pause and take a moment to pray about how God wants you to serve others. Ask Him to reveal things to you.

I Will Set My Thoughts on His Word

In my heart there is no room for others, it is all about me.
Help me to take my eyes off my own desires:
to give warmth to the cold and food to the hungry;
to give drink to the thirsty;
and whatever else Your will requires.
Let there be no other motive but that Your love transpires.

MY PRAYER TO GOD

_____
_____
_____
_____

God revealed to me what I must PUT OFF:
_____

And what I must PUT ON:
_____

5 THINGS I AM THANKFUL FOR

_____
_____
_____
_____
_____
_____

DAY 15

READING & PRAYING

= *Worship*

❦

*Exalt the LORD our God, and worship at His
holy hill; for the LORD our God is holy.*
PSALM 99:9

❖ ❖ ❖

*"But the hour is coming, and now is, when the true
worshipers will worship the Father in spirit and truth;
for the Father is seeking such to worship Him.
God is Spirit, and those who worship Him
must worship in spirit and truth."*
JOHN 4:23-24

❖ ❖ ❖

*For it is written, "You shall worship the LORD your
God, and Him only you shall serve."*
MATTHEW 4:10B

Pause and take a moment to pray about how you are worshiping God. Ask Him to reveal things to you.

I Will Set My Thoughts on His Word

Father, You are Holy, I shall shout Your name.
"Holy, Holy, Holy," I shall proclaim.
Humble me; I want to worship You only, as you have intended.
I shall worship You in truth as Your Word has commanded.
Worshiping You with all my heart, I shall be found
In Your presence as I stand on Holy ground.

MY PRAYER TO GOD

_____
_____
_____
_____

God revealed to me what I must PUT OFF:

_____

And what I must PUT ON:

_____

5 THINGS I AM THANKFUL FOR

_____
_____
_____
_____
_____
_____

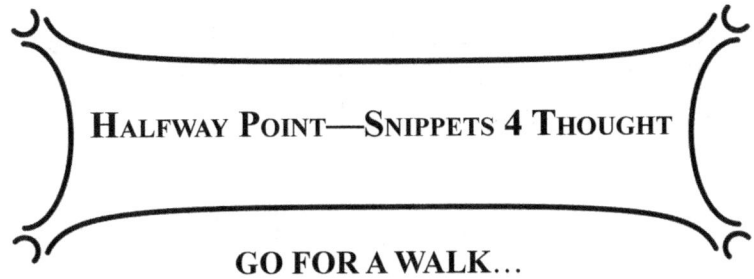

HALFWAY POINT—SNIPPETS 4 THOUGHT

GO FOR A WALK...
It really helps you clear your mind.
It gives you energy.

It is a perfect time to pray. It gives you an opportunity to look at things that God has created. You are able to praise Him for those things. Recognize Him in all His works; example, He created the sun to give us light.

DO SOMETHING POSITIVE...
Intentionally call someone to go have an ice cream,
to go to a movie, or to go to lunch or dinner.
Fellowship with others.

Call, text, or e-mail someone with words of encouragement. Just go and visit and do something special for someone. Serve at your church.

A-I-M...
Be ATTENTIVE to God's Word and take Him at His Word.
Believe that He is faithful and keeps His promises.
Be INTENTIONAL in applying His Word to your life.

You just can't read it...but YOU must live it. Always **MEDITATE** on His Word. Fill your mind with God's commandments, promises and His lovingkindness.

LISTEN TO WORSHIP MUSIC...
You will find that this is a wonderful way to sing to our God, to praise Him and acknowledge Him for who He is. A great way to have your thoughts be immediately turned to Jesus.

MAKE LISTS OF THINGS
YOU WANT TO GET DONE...
Once you cross out something of your list it feels GREAT! You can accomplish things...so don't think you can't.

DAY 16

READING & PRAYING

= *Praise*

*Because Your lovingkindness is better than life,
my lips shall praise You. Thus I will bless You while
I live; I will lift up my hands in Your name.*
PSALM 63:3-4

❖ ❖ ❖

*I will praise You, for I am fearfully and
wonderfully made; marvelous are Your works,
and that my soul knows very well.*

PSALM 139:14

❖ ❖ ❖

*That you may proclaim the praises of Him who called
you out of darkness into His marvelous light.*
1 PETER 2:9B

Pause and take a moment to pray about praising God for all the things He has done for you. Ask Him to reveal things to you.

I Will Set My Thoughts on His Word

With my lips I will praise You for Your awesome works and might.
I shall praise You for the stars, moon, and sun that shine bright.
I will praise You in the morning, noon, and night—
I will praise You for pulling me out of the darkness...
And making my life right.
May my praises always be in Your sight.

MY PRAYER TO GOD

_____
_____
_____
_____

God revealed to me what I must PUT OFF:

_____

And what I must PUT ON:

_____

5 THINGS I AM THANKFUL FOR

_____
_____
_____
_____
_____
_____

READING & PRAYING

= *Reconciliation*

*For if when we were enemies we were reconciled to
God through the death of His Son, much more having
been reconciled, we shall be saved by His life.
And not only that, but we also rejoice in God through
our Lord Jesus Christ, through whom we have
now received the reconciliation.*
ROMANS 5:10-11

*Now all things are of God, who has reconciled us to
Himself through Jesus Christ, and has given us the
ministry of reconciliation, that is, that God was in
Christ reconciling the world to Himself,
not imputing their trespasses to them,
and has committed to us the word of reconciliation.*
2 CORINTHIANS 5:18-19

Pause and take a moment to pray about God's desire to reconcile us to Himself. Ask Him to reveal things to you.

I Will Set My Thoughts on His Word

*Your eyes could not look upon me
because of my sin.
So You arranged a way to end the separation—
Jesus' blood for my restoration.
His death has brought me life that cannot be measured.
Your love for me will always be treasured.*

MY PRAYER TO GOD

_____
_____
_____
_____

God revealed to me what I must PUT OFF:
_____
And what I must PUT ON:
_____

5 THINGS I AM THANKFUL FOR

_____
_____
_____
_____
_____
_____

READING & PRAYING

= *Freedom*

*"For even the Son of man did not come to be served,
but to serve, and to give His life a ransom for many."*
MARK 10:45

*"And you shall know the truth, and the truth shall set
you free...Therefore if the Son makes you free,
you shall be free indeed."*
JOHN 8:32, 36

*There is therefore now no condemnation to those who
are in Christ Jesus, who do not walk according
to the flesh, but according to the Spirit.*
ROMANS 8:1

*For you were bought at a price; therefore glorify God
in your body and in your spirit, which are God's.*
1 CORINTHIANS 6:20

Pause and take a moment to pray about the freedom God has given you. Ask Him to reveal things to you.

I Will Set My Thoughts on His Word

I am redeemed. Jesus, you paid for my sin.
You came and rescued me from the prison I was in.
You are Truth and You set me free,
No more chains because You died on a tree.
You paid the price for me;
a debt I could not pay...
May I use my freedom to praise You night and day.

MY PRAYER TO GOD

_____
_____
_____
_____

God revealed to me what I must PUT OFF:
_____

And what I must PUT ON:
_____

5 THINGS I AM THANKFUL FOR

_____
_____
_____
_____
_____
_____
_____

READING & PRAYING

= *Trust*

Trust in the LORD with all your heart,
and lean not on your own understanding;
in all your ways acknowledge Him
and He shall direct your paths.

PROVERBS 3:5-6

❖ ❖ ❖

Every work of God is pure; He is a shield
to those who put their trust in Him.

PROVERBS 30:5

❖ ❖ ❖

Those who trust in the LORD are like Mount Zion,
which cannot be moved, but abides forever.

PSALM 125:1

Pause and take a moment to pray about your trust in God. Ask Him to reveal things to you.

I Will Set My Thoughts on His Word

Strengthen my heart to trust in You,
That my paths may be formed by Your direction.
You are my hope and my Rock,
I shall not be shaken...for You are my protection.

MY PRAYER TO GOD

_____
_____
_____
_____

God revealed to me what I must PUT OFF:
_____

And what I must PUT ON:
_____

5 THINGS I AM THANKFUL FOR

_____
_____
_____
_____
_____

READING & PRAYING

= *Grace*

For the LORD God is a sun and shield; the LORD will give grace and glory; no good thing will he withhold from those who walk uprightly.
PSALM 84:11

For we do not have a High Priest who cannot sympathize with our weaknesses, but was in all points tempted as we are, yet without sin. Let us therefore come boldly to the throne of grace, that we may obtain mercy and find grace to help in time of need.
HEBREWS 4:15-16

That in the ages to come He might show the exceeding riches of His grace in His kindness toward us in Christ Jesus. For by grace we have been saved through faith, and that not of yourselves; it is the gift of God.
EPHESIANS 2:7-8

Pause and take a moment to pray about God's grace towards you. Ask Him to reveal things to you.

I Will Set My Thoughts on His Word

Ashamed to approach Your throne because of my sin,
Jesus Christ shed His blood so that I could walk in.
Salvation a free gift I don't have to buy,
I shall walk in righteousness; You are my supply.
Open my eyes to Your grace, and remove my blindness.
You are my sun and shield and full of kindness.

MY PRAYER TO GOD

_____
_____
_____
_____

God revealed to me what I must PUT OFF:
_____
And what I must PUT ON:
_____

5 THINGS I AM THANKFUL FOR

_____
_____
_____
_____
_____
_____
_____

READING & PRAYING

= *Mercy*

For You, Lord, are good, and ready to forgive, and abundant in mercy to all those who call upon You.
PSALM 86:5

❖ ❖ ❖

Through the LORD'S mercies we are not consumed, because His compassions fail not. They are new every morning; great is Your faithfulness.
LAMENTATIONS 3:22-23

❖ ❖ ❖

But, God who is rich in mercy because of His great love with which He loved us, even when we were dead in trespasses, made us alive together with Christ (by grace you have been saved).
EPHESIANS 2:4-5

Pause and take a moment to pray about God's mercy towards you. Ask Him to reveal things to you.

I Will Set My Thoughts on His Word

Oh Lord, that I should call upon You daily,
You refrain from harming me, instead You forgive me.
Jesus, You make me alive and give me salvation,
You did not let me be consumed so that I could be free.
You are great in faithfulness and in love,
New every morning are mercies from above.

MY PRAYER TO GOD

_____
_____
_____
_____

God revealed to me what I must PUT OFF:
_____

And what I must PUT ON:
_____

5 THINGS I AM THANKFUL FOR

_____
_____
_____
_____
_____
_____

DAY 22

ARISE IN ME

READING & PRAYING

= Compassion

But He, being full of compassion,
forgave their iniquity, and did not destroy them.
Yes, many a time He turned His anger away
and did not stir up all His wrath.

PSALM 78:38

❖ ❖ ❖

But when He saw the multitudes,
He was moved with compassion for them,
because they were scattered,
like sheep having no shepherd.

MATTHEW 9:36

❖ ❖ ❖

Now as He drew near,
He saw the city and wept over it.

LUKE 19:41

Pause and take a moment to pray about God's compassion towards you. Ask Him to reveal things to you.

I Will Set My Thoughts on His Word

You saw my sufferings and You had deep sorrow,
You forgave me my sins and gave me hope for tomorrow.
You knew I was lost like a sheep going astray.
Be my Shepherd Jesus and lead the way.

MY PRAYER TO GOD

_____
_____
_____
_____

God revealed to me what I must PUT OFF:
_____

And what I must PUT ON:
_____

5 THINGS I AM THANKFUL FOR

_____
_____
_____
_____
_____

READING & PRAYING

= *Comfort*

The LORD will also be a refuge for the oppressed, a refuge in times of trouble.

PSALM 9:9

❖ ❖ ❖

Cast your burden on the LORD, and he shall sustain you; He shall never permit the righteous to be moved.

PSALM 55:22

❖ ❖ ❖

Blessed be the God and Father of our Lord Jesus Christ, the Father of mercies and God of all comfort, who comforts us in all our tribulation, that we may be able to comfort those who are in any trouble, with which we ourselves are comforted by God.

2 CORINTHIANS 1:3-4

Pause and take a moment to pray about the comforts of God. Ask Him to reveal things to you.

I Will Set My Thoughts on His Word

My burdens are many; I feel like I'm drowning.
They are painful, crushing, and overwhelming.
I cast them all on You, for You to carry...
That I may find rest and not be weary.
No matter the trouble, in You I shall find rest.
Jesus, in You there is victory from all my brokenness.

MY PRAYER TO GOD

_____
_____
_____
_____

God revealed to me what I must PUT OFF:
_____

And what I must PUT ON:
_____

5 THINGS I AM THANKFUL FOR

_____
_____
_____
_____
_____
_____
_____

READING & PRAYING

= *Meditation*

*Blessed is the man who walks not in the counsel of the
ungodly, nor stands in the path of sinners, nor sits in
the seat of the scornful; but his delight is in the law of
the LORD, and in His law he mediates day and night.*
PSALM 1:1-2

❖ ❖ ❖

*I will meditate on Your precepts, and contemplate
Your ways. I will delight myself in Your statues;
I will not forget Your word.*
PSALM 119:15-16

❖ ❖ ❖

*Your word I have hidden in my heart, that I might not
sin against You. Blessed are You, O LORD!
Teach me Your statues.*
PSALM 119:11-12

Pause and take a moment to pray about meditating on God's word. Ask Him to reveal things to you.

I Will Set My Thoughts on His Word

When my mind is full of thoughts, I cannot think,
Strengthen me to pick up your Word
for me to contemplate.
May I meditate on Your laws day and night,
May they take effect in my heart and mind and resonate.
Create my path to walk in your ways...
To love Your commandments all of my days.

MY PRAYER TO GOD

_____

_____

_____

_____

God revealed to me what I must PUT OFF:

_____

And what I must PUT ON:

_____

5 THINGS I AM THANKFUL FOR

_____

_____

_____

_____

_____

_____

READING & PRAYING

= *Believing*

But as many as received Him, to them
He gave the right to become children of God,
to those who believe in His name.
JOHN 1:12

❖ ❖ ❖

"Let not your heart be troubled; you believe in God,
believe also in me." ...Jesus said to him,
"I am the way, the truth and the life. No one
comes to the Father except through Me."
JOHN 14:1, 6

❖ ❖ ❖

But these are written that you may believe
that Jesus is the Son of God, and that believing
you may have life in His name.
JOHN 20:31

Pause and take a moment to pray about if you truly are believing in Jesus Christ. Ask Him to reveal things to you.

I Will Set My Thoughts on His Word

In Your name Jesus, I want to believe,
Take away the thoughts that the enemy uses to deceive.
You are the Way and the Life and I want to follow You.
You are the Truth and Your commands I shall do.

MY PRAYER TO GOD

_____
_____
_____
_____

God revealed to me what I must PUT OFF:
_____

And what I must PUT ON:
_____

5 THINGS I AM THANKFUL FOR

_____
_____
_____
_____
_____
_____
_____

READING & PRAYING

= *Contentment*

Not that I speak in regard to need, for I have learned in whatever state I am, to be content.
PHILIPPIANS 4:11

Now godliness with contentment is great gain.
...And having food and clothing
with these we shall be content.
1 TIMOTHY 6:6, 8

Let your conduct be without covetousness;
be content with such things as you have.
For He Himself has said,
"I will never leave you
nor forsake you."
HEBREWS 13:5

Pause and take a moment to pray about being content with what you have. Ask Him to reveal things to you.

I Will Set My Thoughts on His Word

In whatever circumstance I am in;
Help me to be satisfied.
I shall not desire what others have,
What I need You have supplied.
You are always with me wherever I go...
You are more than enough; this I shall come to know.

MY PRAYER TO GOD

_____
_____
_____
_____

God revealed to me what I must PUT OFF:
_____

And what I must PUT ON:
_____

5 THINGS I AM THANKFUL FOR

_____
_____
_____
_____
_____
_____
_____

READING & PRAYING

= *Perseverance*

And not only that, but we also glory in tribulations, knowing that tribulation produces perseverance; and perseverance, character; and character, hope.

ROMANS 5:3-4

❖ ❖ ❖

Rejoicing in hope, patient in tribulation, continuing steadfastly in prayer.

ROMANS 12:12

❖ ❖ ❖

Not that I have already attained, or am already perfected; but I press on, that I may lay hold of that for which Christ Jesus has also laid hold of me. Brethren, I do not count myself to have apprehended; but one thing I do, forgetting those things which are behind and reaching forward to those things which are ahead, I press toward the goal for the prize of the upward call of God in Christ Jesus.

PHILIPPIANS 3:12-14

Pause and take a moment to pray about how you will persevere in your circumstances. Ask Him to reveal things to you.

I Will Set My Thoughts on His Word

Help me to press on no matter what I am going through. You are building my character...giving me hope in You.

I must forget the past and set my mind on the goal. Being perfected in Jesus Christ is good for my soul.

MY PRAYER TO GOD

_____
_____
_____
_____

God revealed to me what I must PUT OFF:

_____

And what I must PUT ON:

_____

5 THINGS I AM THANKFUL FOR

_____
_____
_____
_____
_____
_____

READING & PRAYING

= *Righteousness*

*Righteousness and justice
are the foundation of Your throne;
mercy and truth go before Your face.*
PSALM 89:14

❖ ❖ ❖

*But, seek first the kingdom of God
and His righteousness,
and all these things
shall be added to you.*
MATTHEW 6:33

❖ ❖ ❖

*But in every nation whoever fears Him
and works righteousness
is accepted by Him.*
ACTS 10:35

Pause and take a moment to pray about living a righteous life. Ask Him to reveal things to you.

I Will Set My Thoughts on His Word

You are a Righteous, Holy and Just God and our King.
With You there is no partiality; You always do the right thing.

Help me to always do what is right in Your sight.
Jesus, keep me strong for I can only do things in Your might.

MY PRAYER TO GOD

_____
_____
_____
_____

God revealed to me what I must PUT OFF:

_____

And what I must PUT ON:

_____

5 THINGS I AM THANKFUL FOR

_____
_____
_____
_____
_____
_____
_____

READING & PRAYING

= *Patience*

*But You, O Lord, are a God full of compassion,
and gracious, longsuffering and
abundant in mercy and truth.*
PSALM 86:15

*Love suffers long and is kind; love does not envy;
love does not parade itself, is not puffed up; does not
behave rudely, does not seek its own, is not provoked,
thinks no evil; does not rejoice in iniquity, but rejoices
in the truth; bears all things, believes all things.*
1 CORINTHIANS 13:4-7

*The Lord is not slack concerning His promise, as
some count slackness, but is longsuffering toward us,
not willing that any should perish but that
all should come to repentance.*
2 PETER 3:9

Pause and take a moment to pray about God's patience with you and your patience towards others. Ask Him to reveal things to you.

I Will Set My Thoughts on His Word

Father God, fill me with the compassion that is in Your heart,
With the love that You had for us from the start.
Let me love others instead of complaining and being moody,
I will not seek my own but only rejoice in Your beauty.
You are longsuffering towards us and want us to repent.
You don't want any of us to perish, this is why Jesus was sent.

MY PRAYER TO GOD

_____
_____
_____
_____

God revealed to me what I must PUT OFF:
_____

And what I must PUT ON:
_____

5 THINGS I AM THANKFUL FOR

_____
_____
_____
_____
_____
_____

READING & PRAYING

= *Overcome*

*"These things I have spoken to you, that in Me
you may have peace. In the world you will have
tribulation; but be of good cheer,
I have overcome the world."*
JOHN 16:33

*Who is he who overcomes the world, but he who
believes that Jesus is the Son of God?*
1 JOHN 5:5

*But those who wait on the LORD shall renew their
strength; they shall mount up with wings like eagles,
they shall run and not be weary,
they shall walk and not faint.*
ISAIAH 40:31

Pause and take a moment to pray and ask God for strength to overcome. Ask Him to reveal things to you.

I Will Set My Thoughts on His Word

Jesus, You overcame the greatest pain and suffering of all,
In my tribulations and battles of my mind, help me to stand tall.

I will wait for You, O LORD for strength to press on,
You overcame the world, because of this it is You I rest upon.

MY PRAYER TO GOD

_____
_____
_____
_____

God revealed to me what I must PUT OFF:
_____

And what I must PUT ON:
_____

5 THINGS I AM THANKFUL FOR

_____
_____
_____
_____
_____
_____

DAY 31

READING & PRAYING

A Heavenly Father

"I will be a Father to you, and you shall be My sons and daughters," says the LORD Almighty.
2 CORINTHIANS 6:18

And the LORD, He is the One who goes before You,
He will be with you,
He will not leave you nor forsake you;
do not fear nor be dismayed.
DEUTERONOMY 31:8

When my father and my mother forsake me,
Then the LORD will take care of me.
PSALM 27:10

Pause and take a moment to pray and ask yourself if you truly seek God as your Father. Ask Him to reveal things to you.

I Will Set My Thoughts on His Word

*I thought I was alone with no one around.
I searched Your scriptures and a Father I found.*

*I shall not be concerned or full of worry.
You take care of me always; this will be my story.*

MY PRAYER TO GOD

_____
_____
_____
_____

God revealed to me what I must PUT OFF:
_____

And what I must PUT ON:
_____

5 THINGS I AM THANKFUL FOR

_____
_____
_____
_____
_____

IN CONCLUSION

I pray that taking one day at a time to focus on God has helped you to direct your thoughts from your circumstances to that of God and all His goodness. Keep focusing on the God of the universe and His righteousness and He will give you all that you need. Jesus tells us in Matthew 6:33, "But seek first the kingdom of God and His righteousness, and all these things shall be added to you." Seek Him through His word and through prayer. Be about your Father's business.

Remember that He is always by your side. He knows all your pains and all of your hurts. He knows all of the circumstances that surround you. He knows everything about you. He is a God Who heals. He heals our broken spirit. He heals our broken relationships. Jeremiah 33:3 "Call to Me, and I will answer you, and show you great and mighty things, which you do not know."

Remember God's love towards you. No one can take His love from you…it is forever.

In Romans 8:37-39 we find:

> *"Yet, in all these things we are more than conquerors through Him who loved us. For I am persuaded that neither death nor life, nor angels nor principalities nor powers, nor things present nor things to come, nor height*

nor depth, nor any other created thing, shall be able to separate us from the love of God which is in Christ Jesus our Lord."

REMEMBER...

Wow...not even the enemy who tries daily can separate you from God!

Jesus gives beauty for ashes.

Be consumed by His love.

LASTLY...

When God says He loves you...
He loves you—unconditionally.

When God says He forgives you...
He forgives you—you are free.

When God says He will never leave you
nor forsake you...
You will never—be alone.

...In Him we Live and Move and Have Our Being.

~ PRAYERS & NOTES ~

_____

_____

_____

_____

_____

_____

_____

_____

_____

_____

_____

_____

_____

_____

_____

_____

_____

_____

www.ingramcontent.com/pod-product-compliance
Lightning Source LLC
Chambersburg PA
CBHW071337130626
46556CB00004B/1929